A Spirit of Giving

Written by David R. Collins

Illustrated by Susan Hall

BROADMAN PRESS
Nashville, Tennessee

4242-38
ISBN: 0-8054-4238-3

Dewey Decimal Classification: JF
Subject heading: CHRISTMAS STORIES//
CHRISTIAN LIFE

Printed in the United States of America.

"Oh, this is hopeless!"

Maribeth Carter plopped back in her chair. Before her on the kitchen table sat the results of two weeks' work. Ever since Maribeth had heard of the Christmas project contest at school, she had thought of nothing else.

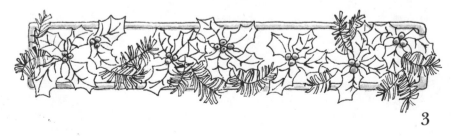

"I'm going to win that contest," she had told herself over and over. "I've just got to."

Each day after school Maribeth had raced home to continue working on her project for the contest. She liked her idea. It was a small cardboard Nativity scene. Carefully she had designed and cut a small shoe box so it would look like a stable. On another piece of cardboard she had drawn the figures who would be standing near the manger. There was Mary and Joseph and a few shepherds. Next came the Wise Men. They had far to travel to find the new Savior of the world. Maribeth put them away from the manger. She pretended they were still traveling. Finally, there were the gentle animals of the stable.

And then there was the baby Jesus. Again and again Maribeth had struggled to draw the tiny figure who would lie in the cardboard manger. Now she was finished.

For several moments Maribeth stared silently at the Nativity scene. Something was wrong. But what? Maribeth looked closely at each standing figure. She made sure the small cardboard brace on the back of each figure was tightly pasted.

7

"Why, you've finished!"

Maribeth had not heard her mother come into the kitchen.

"Yes, I've finished. But just look at it, Mother. It's so drab and plain. It's not the way I wanted it to be at all."

"Why, Maribeth, I think it's a beautiful Nativity scene," Mrs. Carter answered. "It's easy to see you spent a lot of time making it. I think it would look lovely on the table in the living room."

Maribeth shook her head. It was just like Mother to make such a suggestion to try and make her feel better. Mother didn't really understand. That day at lunchtime Jeff Wilkins had told everyone about the battery his father was putting in his project to make it move. And Laurie Johnson was sure to have a better project. She was always so good in art.

Slowly Maribeth put the cardboard pieces of her Nativity scene inside the stable. She stared at each piece. She wished she could have made each one more beautiful. If only each small figure could become as beautiful as the story itself . . . .

"Hurry up, Maribeth," her mother said. "I need the table so I can get supper ready. You'll want to get to bed early since the big contest is tomorrow."

Maribeth nodded and carried the cardboard stable into her room. Yes, she would go to bed early. All the projects had to be set up before school started. If she could get to school early enough, maybe she could get a good place to display her project. There might be at least *one* place where her project would look better than anywhere else. It was worth a try.

Maribeth did get to school early the next morning. But there were others who had come even earlier. Miss Clark, the teacher, was standing at the classroom doorway.

"Well, Maribeth, you are here bright and early this morning. I hope you can find a place on one of the tables to display your project."

Maribeth looked at the five tables set aside for the Christmas projects. Spotting a small open space, she hurried to it and began setting up her small Nativity scene. As she worked, she tried not to notice the other displays. But she could not help it. So many had bright colorful ornaments. And there was Jeff Wilkins with a *moving* figure of Santa Claus!

15

16

"Miss Clark, may I put my star on this hook?"

At the sound of Laurie Johnson's voice, Maribeth turned around. Her eyes widened at the sight of a big, golden-foiled star Laurie was holding. Tiny sequins sparkled on the star.

"Yes, Laurie, that would be fine," Miss Clark answered. "It looks like we really have some lovely projects this year. I'm sure the judges won't have an easy time making a decision."

Maribeth watched Laurie hang her golden star. How beautiful it sparkled in the morning sunlight. Sadly Maribeth glanced down at her own project. It looked even more plain than it had before.

"While the judges are here, I want all of you to be reading at your desks," Miss Clark announced. "I will tell you their decision as soon as they have finished."

Quickly the boys and girls hurried to their desks. In a few minutes, Miss Clark walked up and down the aisles, making certain everyone was reading.

"S-s-s-t, Miss Clark?"

A whisper from the doorway caught Miss Clark's attention, and she walked briskly across the room. Miss Clark stepped out of the room for a minute. When she came back, three men were with her.

"Those must be the judges!" Jeff Wilkins mumbled ahead to Maribeth.

Maribeth tried to read, but she couldn't. Her eyes kept watching the three judges as they examined the projects. Each judge carried a small notebook and wrote things down in it. Now and then, one judge would whisper to another.

Maribeth squirmed in her desk. Looking around, she discovered she was not the only one watching the judges. Every boy and girl in the room was watching.

"Oh, I do so want to win!" Jeff whispered. "Don't you, Maribeth?"

Maribeth nodded. She was slightly annoyed by such a silly question. Of course, she wanted to win. Didn't everyone in the room? How could anyone ask such a . . . .

21

Suddenly Maribeth felt her stomach churning. It felt the same way it did when she had had the flu last year. The judges were standing right above her Nativity scene. One of the men bent over, looking carefully inside the manger she had made. What could be taking the judges so long?

Finally, the three men turned and walked to Miss Clark's desk. After what seemed like an hour, the teacher stood.

24

"Class, I know how eager you all are to find out the winner of the contest," she smiled. "The judges want to let you know how fine they thought the projects were. It was not easy to pick a winner, but they have managed to do it."

Again Maribeth squirmed in her desk. She closed her eyes, hoping to hear her name called.

"The winner . . . ," Miss Clark announced, "is Laurie Johnson."

Laurie Johnson let out a surprised and joyful squeal. As Maribeth opened her eyes, she saw a few girls jump up and run to Laurie's desk. Maribeth joined them. For just a moment she forgot her own disappointment. But as soon as she returned to her desk, she felt her stomach churning again.

As Miss Clark turned to speak to one of the judges, Maribeth glanced over at Laurie's golden star. It deserved to win she decided. It *was* beautiful. But even knowing that could not take away her own disappointment.

"We'll be needing a few of the tables today," Miss Clark nodded. "Perhaps a few of you might put your projects together so we will have more space."

Slowly Maribeth got up and walked over to her Nativity scene. She started to put the small cardboard figures into the cardboard stable when she noticed one of the judges standing beside her.

"Is this your project?" he asked.

Maribeth nodded, picking up the figures more rapidly.

"I was wondering if you would let me use it over the Christmas holidays?"

Maribeth was puzzled. Lend her Nativity scene? Why?

"You see, I have a very small church a few blocks from here," the man said. "The people who come to it do not have much money. We cannot afford to buy a Nativity scene for the church. But yours—yours would be perfect. I could put it on the table at the front of the church."

29

Maribeth could not believe her ears. She swallowed deeply.

"You—you want to use my Nativity scene in—in your church?" she whispered.

"Yes, if you are willing. You would be giving us a fine Christmas gift if you would say yes."

"But—but it is so simple . . . so plain."

"And that is *why* it is so beautiful. That is how the baby Jesus came to us. You have helped remind us."

Maribeth stared down at the small cardboard figures. Somehow they looked different than they had before. Maybe there really was beauty in something that looked so simple and plain on the outside. Maybe other people would feel that beauty, too.

"Oh, yes, of course you may have them. I will come to see them in your church."

"Good. I know the people will have a better Christmas because of your kindness," the man smiled.

"I hope so," Maribeth nodded. "This will be the happiest Christmas *I* have ever had!"